Eloise's Christmas story

Stick your favorite picture here

Special Message

Eloise

Christmas is coming, it's no nursery rhyme,

It happens each year at the same time.

There are lots of things to arrange and do,
But, you have so much fun ahead of you.

Eloise

The season is magical, and special you know,

Santa's working hard at his home in the snow.

At the North Pole the elves are all helping too,
To prepare all the presents for children like you.

The reindeer are waiting to pull Santa's slay,
So the gifts are delivered by Christmas Day.

Eloise

Santa keeps a list of good kids and bad,

If your on the good list, you will not be sad.

I know you're excited, and each day is long,
But we'll pass the time singing fun Christmas songs.

We'll hang up the tinsel, baubles, and wreath,
Then place the Christmas tree, and put gifts beneath.

Eloise

We could make snow men and have snowball fights,
Skate on the ice, drink hot chocolate at night.

We'll find a big moose, and invite it to tea,
So it can enjoy Christmas with you and me.

On the night before Christmas, we'll leave Santa treats,
Like a glass of milk and some cookies to eat.

Eloise

On Christmas morning, check under the tree,
You'll find out how amazing a Christmas can be.

Merry Christmas

Printed in Great Britain
by Amazon

33204963R00018